DO I NEED A LAWYER?

VOL. 1: TRAFFIC TICKETS AND PETTY CRIMES

DAVID N. PAULY

Copyright (C) 2019 David N. Pauly

Layout design and Copyright (C) 2019 by Creativia

Published 2019 by Creativia (www.creativia.org)

Edited by Marilyn Wagner

Cover art by Cover Mint

All rights reserved. No part of this book may be reproduced or transmitted in any form or by any means, electronic or mechanical, including photocopying, recording, or by any information storage and retrieval system, without the author's permission.

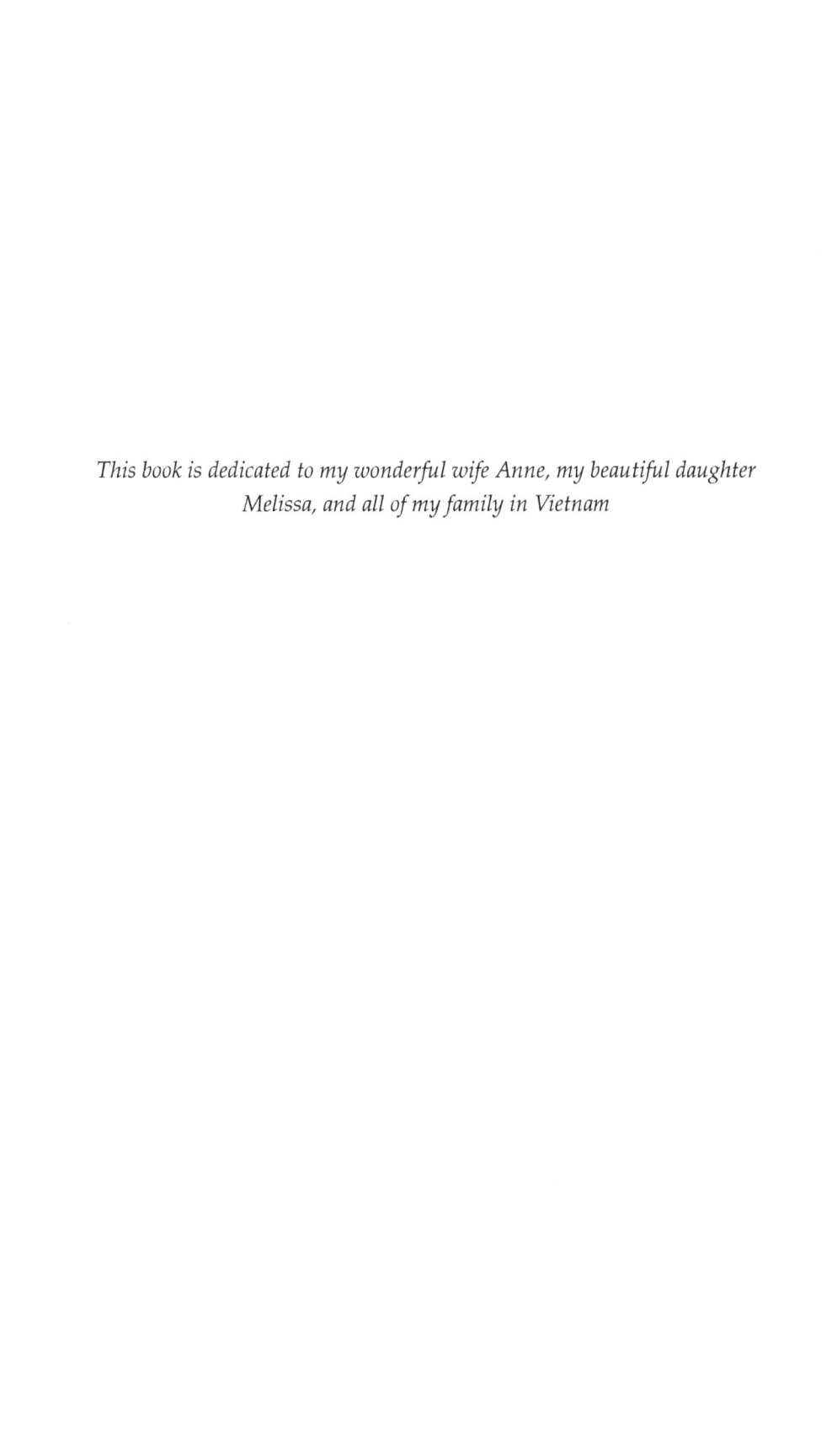

This book is dedicated to my wonderful wife Anne, my beautiful daughter Melissa, and all of my family in Vietnam

ACKNOWLEDGMENTS

This book would not have occurred to me to write without the inspiration and support of my fellow author, Noel Eastwood, for which I am ever grateful. All of my partners at Creativia have been wonderful, as well as the support I have received from friends and colleagues. Finally, I have to credit my past clients, fellow lawyers, judges, and law enforcement, who taught me how to practice law in the real world.

INTRODUCTION

Yes, you do, if not now then eventually, you will need one of us to help you with something. It might be as innocuous as drafting a will, or as terrifying as defending you from death row, it just depends on your choices. This is the first in a series about the law, based upon my legal experiences as a lawyer for over 25 years, filled with real-life examples from representing over 5,000 clients, I will cover the most common criminal offenses that people commit in this volume, which should help many of you.

Crimes can be as minor as a speeding ticket, up to multiple homicides, chances are that at some point you will commit some sort of crime. When that day comes, do not make your 2nd mistake by trying to handle your self-created mess on your own. Your 1st mistake was committing a crime in the first place, by the way.

WHY DON'T I SUGGEST THAT YOU HANDLE IT ON YOUR OWN?

Because the law can be as complicated as medicine, and without a proper education, home remedies can only take you so far. So, if you wind up staring at a police officer without a sense of humor, call a lawyer as soon as possible: **Do Not Represent Yourself!** Thankfully,

Judges try and prevent most people from representing themselves in court; the main exception is in traffic court and some minor charges that don't carry mandatory jail time. But, even some of these small offenses have nasty consequences, such as being barred from many different jobs, or being prevented from taking out student loans, and one specific offense usually leads to divorce.

Now jail is an obvious outcome that most people would like to prevent, and unless you have done something particularly serious, your lawyer will probably get you some sort of probation for whatever dumb thing you decided to do.

BUT WHAT ABOUT NOT BEING ABLE TO GET CERTAIN JOBS, THIS MAKES NO SENSE TO ME, YOU SAY.

If you commit a crime that raises questions about your honesty, or integrity, it will haunt you forever. For example, on your 21st birthday, you decide to steal a really expensive bottle of scotch from the local liquor store. You get caught and if it's less than $300-$500 dollars, you get a shoplifting ticket. If it's more than $500, you will be arrested and charged with either misdemeanor or felony theft. Stealing is dishonest, whether it's just a ticket, or a criminal conviction and many high paying jobs insist that their members are honest, or at least have not gotten caught yet.

So, even the aforementioned shoplifting ticket will prevent you from going to law school. Yes, I know we have a terrible reputation, but remember once we are lawyers then we can steal but not before, we have to be educated, regulated thieves. You can also forget about politics other than anything at a community level. Working in any field which requires any sort of security clearance is also out of the question. In this hypothetical scenario, one stupid move, probably while you were already drunk, carries major repercussions. Just ask Wynona Ryder how well her acting career went after getting busted for shoplifting.

WHAT ABOUT SCHOOL, HOW CAN A CRIME STOP ME THERE?

The easiest example is drug possession, even just a joint, if you live in a jurisdiction where pot is still illegal; a conviction is enough to ruin your life. In the United States, if you are convicted or plead guilty of possessing any illegal drug, **you are ineligible for Federal Guaranteed student loans of any kind forever.** Now, let that sink in for a moment. You get busted for a joint, and unless you can pay for school yourself, you will be working in the food service industry, or if you're lucky, in a trade like welding forever. As you will see shortly, a lawyer can make all of these nasty consequences disappear; you just have to pay us, and sometimes it's a lot, to clean up your mess. If you are interested in the humorous side of practicing law, where I clean up lots of messes, please read my memoir series, "Expensive Janitor."

So now you know why you want a lawyer for a crime with consequences, but what about speeding tickets, surely I can handle those on my own right?

Nope, not a chance.

If you request a court date, your lawyer can help in big ways. First, the cop that stopped you only shows up about half of the time to traffic court. Why? Because court dates are always scheduled on a cop's day off so that the cop is not wasting his assigned duty shift by being in court. Now no one likes to lose their day off, particularly if it's connected to a weekend, holiday, or any other time where the days can be connected together. So, quite often, the cop does not show up to traffic court

WELL, I CAN REQUEST A COURT DATE AND TAKE MY CHANCES THAT THE COP WILL NOT SHOW UP, RIGHT?

Wrong. If the cop does not show up, the court most likely will not dismiss the ticket but instead, reschedule it for another time, and you are more likely to have the cop show up that time. Worse, if you guess wrong, and the cop does show up, you will be convicted unless you have a witness, other than yourself who can testify how fast you were actually going.

Why?

Because the judge believes that the officer does not have the self interest to lie that an accused speeder does, and will actually tell the truth, after he has sworn an oath to do so. We will discuss this fallacy later, but trust me, I have been in traffic court more times than I care to recount, and the only people who get out of the ticket have their lawyer with them. This will get covered in the first chapter of this book. I will then describe other crimes, criminal procedure, how trials work, and how we lawyers get you out of your own mess.

WHY IS THE LAW SO MESSED UP THAT I HAVE TO HIRE A LAWYER FOR ANYTHING THAT I DO WRONG?

An excellent question as the law should be simple and straight forward. Lawyers, however, are predatory by nature and always hungry for more money. Since the time of Hammurabi's Codex, which is a black granite stele, in the basement of the Louvre with his laws carved into the rock in about 1800 BC, lawyers have made the law more and more complicated, to make sure that we have guaranteed employment.

By now, you might be feeling negative about crime, and the fact that it truly never pays. This assumption could not be further from the truth. Crime pays quite well, it covers my mortgage, utilities and car payments with a little left over, so let's have a look into the dark, mysterious, dangerous and preposterously stupid world of crime.

CHAPTER 1
SPEEDING TICKETS

So, you are not paying attention while driving home from work, and suddenly there are flashers behind you approaching at a high rate of speed. You look at your speedometer, and you were doing 10 miles an hour over. You pull over immediately, and you get out your insurance, your license and registration, well before the cop arrives at your window.

Why?

Because sadly lots of cops get shot or attacked by people with serious arrest warrants out for them, so the cop gets really uncomfortable seeing you rummaging around in your glove box for your paperwork. So get it out ahead of time.

Now, the cop is going to ask you two questions, the first is a variation on the same theme, "Do you know why I pulled you over?" The answer to this question needs to be **honest, I repeat, HONEST!!!** The cop did not choose you at random because he did not like the color of your skin or the fact that you were driving a beater. Oops, technically that's not true if you live in an expensive white neighborhood, like where I grew up, the cops are paid to profile everyone that they see to make certain that they have any business, besides planning a felony, for being in the rich white town.

However, let's assume that profiling in your case is not an issue. So, when he or she asks "Do you know why I stopped you?" you say the following in the most apologetic tone, "Probably because I was speeding. I am very sorry officer; I was not paying attention to how fast I was going." Now, having used this reply personally, I can tell you that right now, you have a 50/50 chance of the cop saying in a surprised tone of voice.

"Wow, you are the first honest person that I have stopped all day. If I let you go without a ticket, will you be more careful?"

"Of course, officer: sorry to put you through any trouble."

At that point, you have avoided the need for me or any of my kind. Congratulations you are home free. Most people, however, are neither clever, much less honest with the cop. The cops hear all sorts of Denials from drivers who are lying through their teeth. Some of these are: "I was not going that fast," "my speedometer is broken", and the worst, one "Hey Officer I don't believe you, I want to see the radar gun." If you choose this pathway, you can forget getting out of this one without help straight away.

After Denial come the Excuses, "I am running late to work/pick up the kids/watch the Cowboys game, etc." Excuses never work, unless it's a real emergency, such as you are a doctor rushing to surgery, your child is in the car seat and delirious with fever, or some other real crisis that the officer will believe and have sympathy for you. Here is a great example of an excellent excuse.

I was representing a guy for a car accident case, where he was the victim, but in a separate incident, he saw the flashers right behind him, as he was driving over 100 mph in his truck through Tijeras Canyon down to Albuquerque. He did not slow down, so the cop pulled alongside his truck and used the speaker on the roof of his patrol unit to demand that my client pull over immediately. My client raised his Volunteer Fireman helmet and pointed ahead to the large plume of smoke coming from a fire down in the Bosque scrub forest that was rapidly spreading out of control. The officer then said over the speaker, "Get Behind Me!" and kept his flashers on and cleared a way through the cars so that my client could literally rush to a fire. Now that's the kind of excuse/explanation that will actually work. Anything else, not so much.

Now there is one other way to get out of a ticket that is totally incorrect, sexist, and probably immoral but it usually works; flirt with the cop. Now ninety percent of cops are men, and like all of us men, we can be easily distracted by a pretty female face, cleavage is even better, into letting you off the hook/cutting you a break. How much flirting you want to do, is entirely up to you, but let me say this. **Hot pretty women never appear in traffic court, never!** Other crimes where the officer has less discretion, yes anyone can get arrested, but not for traffic tickets.

SO, WHAT DO YOU MEAN BY FLIRTING?

I am a straight white male, who can barely make small talk, so I do not have the foggiest idea on how to flirt, but from reputable hot chicks, I can lay it out for you, pun intended. First, while the cop is running your license plates to make certain that you are not part of ISIS' plans to blow something up, unbutton your blouse, put on lipstick, and do anything else to make yourself look more attractive. Next, the conversation starts out as an apology, and then when you are reaching for your license and insurance, which you have left on the passenger seat, you present it to the office with a hair flip and a giggle. Eye batting is now necessary and playing with one of your buttons on your shirt is a big plus. If you have the legs for it, and they are visible, the following will also work. Push your seat back as far as it can go, and put your feet up on the glove box. If the cop says anything about your feet on the dashboard, you say that 'My back hurts, it's a little stiff, what should I do about it?'

At this point, if its summer time and you flirt properly, you are good to go. If the cop is stubborn but is smiling at you, offer to give him your phone number. Not your real number genius, but something else, and write it down for him on a piece of paper with your first name, a smiling emoji, and the last words say, 'Call Me,'

Ok, yes, that whole bit was gross, sexist, inflammatory, ad nauseum, I get that. But this is a book about how to get out of a ticket, and as Katy Perry infamously said about a similar situation and how her looks got her out of a jam, she said and I quote, 'If you've got it, use it.' Truer words have never been spoken. But, presuming that flirting will not work, because, you're a guy, an unattractive or older woman, or you got stopped by a straight female cop and you are not a male model, you need to continue reading.

So, back to you sitting on the side of the road, where the officer is not feeling charitable by your admission of guilt, or pissed off and cynical that you lied to him if you denied you were speeding, or your explanation did not pass muster.

SO NOW WHAT DO YOU DO?

ASK TO GO TO COURT! I will say that again, **ASK TO GO TO COURT!** In most states, you have the choice to ask for a court date or agree to pay the fine within 5 days of the ticket date. Not in New Mexico. You have to decide right there on the spot if you want to go to court or pay the fine. Trust me you want to go to court, even if you are foolish enough to represent yourself.

Now the officer may be dishonest, and try and tell you that if agree to pay the fine, you can send a letter to the Department of Motor Vehicles, requesting that no points be put on your license. This is a bald-faced lie, it's not true, and it won't work. This is just the cop's way of getting you to pay for your ticket. Despite what is publicly said robotically by police departments around the country, that there are no ticket or arrest quotas for police officers this is another bald-faced lie. I have friends in different branches of law enforcement in New Mexico, and several other states throughout the country, and off the record, each of them told me that they are evaluated in job performance reviews as to how many tickets they give out each month, how many arrests they make, and how many of those arrests result in convictions or guilty pleas.

All of those statistics are used to determine which officer gets promoted from an ordinary patrolman or deputy to a sergeant; the first step up the promotion ladder. Trust me when I say that when you are speaking with a sergeant in court, particularly a young one, they are gung-ho, they stop everyone for anything that they can think of and kiss a lot of asses, their captain's, the prosecutors', and even the judges'. The sergeant is aware that the more tickets/arrests his subordinates make, the closer he is to making lieutenant.

Presuming the officer actually checks the court date box, rather than telling you that he did, you are good to go until your court date. This gives you plenty of time to find a lawyer to represent you in court, and you should use this time wisely. Most traffic cases will not cost you that much money, about $300-400 dollars in legal fees, so it won't break your piggy bank.

BUT THE FINE IS ONLY $109.00 AND I HAVE TO TAKE TIME OFF FROM WORK, AND GOING TO COURT IS A BIG HASSLE SO I SHOULD JUST PAY IT, RIGHT?

No!

While your points have merit, you need to consider the hidden costs of that traffic ticket. In New Mexico, you get a total of 10 points on your license for a 2-year period, and different tickets have different points. 1-9 miles over the limit is 2 points, while 10-19 is 4 points and 20 and over you can expect a misdemeanor criminal charge, such as Careless Driving or Reckless Driving, which carry 6 points and 10 points respectively. Also, the misdemeanors expose you to potential jail time as well.

WELL, I HAVE BEEN DRIVING FOR TEN YEARS AND THIS IS MY FIRST TICKET, I CAN SUCK UP THE 2 POINTS, PAY THE $109 BUCKS AND BE ON MY WAY, RIGHT?

Not so fast my friend, now we need to take your car insurance into account. One of the cute little fine print boxes you agree to in that huge amount of paperwork that your insurer sends you, that you will never read, allows them to search your driving history at will. Sooner or later, they will find out that you were speeding, and ratchet up your premium by a minimum of 25% to 50%, for the next 2-4 years. As an example, if you are paying $100/month in insurance premiums, you will now be paying an extra $25/month, which turns out to be $600-$1200 total. I will do the math for you; you are going to shell out a minimum of $700 dollars by paying your ticket, and the insurer has one last nasty surprise lurking for you if you are not careful. If you get a second ticket within their 2-4 year period, they will probably cancel your policy, forcing you to get one of those high-risk policies from some dirt-bag company like "Dairyland", "Phoenix Indemnity", "Liberty Mutual", or the worst of them all, "Nevada General". You can plan on paying about $300/month instead of the $100/month example that I have used in this example for your insurance.

Now you are starting to see that spending $300-400 on a lawyer is actually a wise investment, particularly if you drive for a living, such as a cabbie, delivery guy, long haul trucker, or even a government job which requires you to have a completely clear license. Here is another example.

My friend, let's call her "Jane" to protect the innocent, is the paramour of my best friend "Jerry", not his real name either, and she was working with a security clearance at the Top Secret Sandia National Labs, when she got stopped on base by the Sandia Base police for only doing 5 miles over the limit. If convicted, she was going to lose her right to drive on the base, much less onto the base, for the next 2 years, making it literally impossible to get to work. Plus the ticket would be sent to her supervisor and she would lose out on 2 years seniority for her next promotion. Pretty nasty consequences for such a minor offense, wouldn't you say? Thankfully, Jane had listened to me and requested a court day, and I filed my Entry of Appearance with the Federal Magistrate Court. Two pleasant phone calls later with a very nice prosecutor got the ticket reduced to a verbal warning, no fine, no bad results, nada.

Plus, as Jane was a good friend, there was no charge for taking care of this. If you had been in Jane's shoes and were simply one of my regular paying clients, I think that you would agree that $400 would have been a very cheap alternative to the contrary.

BUT HOW DO YOU LAWYERS GET US OUT OF OUR SPEEDING TICKETS YOU ASK?

Well, here is your answer.

First, once you have a lawyer on your case, the court and anyone involved from the prosecution side will take you much more seriously. So, if the cop does not show up on your case, nearly all the time, the matter will be dismissed unless the cop has called in with a valid excuse. The reason for this is that the prosecutor is not representing the City, County or State for the ticket, the officer is. Therefore, there is no one to speak up for the cop if they are not there, and as Woody Allen famously said, "Ninety percent of life is showing up."

Now, what happens if the cop shows up for your ticket? That's when we make our money. In most jurisdictions, the only thing that the cop cares about is not losing their little case. Their ego gets involved quite easily, and the last thing that they will ever admit to is that they made a mistake. So, with proper handling, your lawyer can make a deal with the cop that keeps your record clean.

The first and best deal is called a Defense Continuance, whereby you and the cop agreed that the case will be continued (postponed) for a set period of time, 90-180 days is the usual time period, and then the case will be dismissed. This does two things, first, it keeps the ticket off of your record, and if it does appear, it will show up as dismissed, which means you can tell anyone down the road if they are interested in it, that the cop did not have a case. The second thing it does is keep you from having any court costs handed to you that you have to pay. Court costs are usually less than a hundred dollars, but hey, every little bit counts.

To get a Defense Continuance, your lawyer generally explains that you have a clean driving record, that you acknowledge your guilt, and that you have already paid out a lot on the case by hiring a lawyer. Most of the time this will be enough, but sometimes, the cop wants an additional penalty, and that's where the charitable contribution comes in. Say the cop wants you to cough up a hundred bucks to a charity as an additional penalty. Guess what, you agree to it and donate money to whatever charity the cop likes, it's usually Crime Stoppers, or a drug prevention program, but hey, this will close the deal.

If the cop does not want to agree to this, your lawyer's next step is to ask if the cop will agree to a guilty plea with a 90-180-day deferment. At the end of that deferment, if you do not re-offend, then the court will dismiss the ticket. This allows the cop to add your "conviction" to their statistics, and if they are low on points that month, this usually happens. It also happens when you the client, were a real pain in the ass to the cop when he or she stopped you.

It never pays to be rude to the cops, never. It's like being rude to your parents when you have done something wrong when you are a child, you never win and it only makes things worse.

Let's say, however, that the cop is really focused on you and wants you convicted. The next thing I try is increasing the charitable contribution, offer to send you to Driver Improvement School, or even "volunteer" you to do community service. Driver Improvement School, also known as Defensive Driving Class, is a one-day class held on a Saturday, and essentially teaches you the same things that you already know, like not to speed. While allegedly educational, its real value to the criminal justice system is that it really hammers the point home that you screwed up. This is because it ruins a perfectly good Saturday for you, and will cost you a hundred bucks or so.

Every now and then, however, the cop flat out won't budge, and that's when your lawyer has to try the case in front of the judge to try and get you off. This can go one of two ways, one of which is if you and the judge get along very well, you can simply plea "No Contest" which means you do not deny the charge, but do not admit to the charge either. The judge will usually agree to your lawyer's request for one of the resolutions, as described above, which does not record a conviction, apply a fine, or post any points on to your driving record.

If your lawyer does not know the judge well, the case will have to go to trial. Unless your lawyer has a very public reputation, you will not know which judge, if any that they get along with, until you ask them during your free consultation.

YOU SHOULD ALWAYS GET YOUR POTENTIAL LAWYER'S OPINION ON YOUR ASSIGNED JUDGE.

If your lawyer disparages (criticizes) the judge and says how horrible they are, you should probably consult another lawyer and see if this is true or if your lawyer just does not get along with them personally.

Assume for a moment that your lawyer gets on well with the judge, all sorts of wonderful things can happen. An excellent example of knowing the judge is when my wife Anne got stopped for speeding on a rural road in the East Mountains of New Mexico. My daughter, Melissa was two and a half, and right in the middle of the "Terrible Twos", and if you are a parent, you know what I am talking about.

Melissa was screaming and throwing a fit, along with throwing her pink monkey "Bobby" from the back car seat, and Anne was losing her temper and began speeding on a deserted road to get Melissa to childcare as soon as possible. The road was deserted, except for a Sherriff's Deputy hiding his cruiser behind a Juniper bush looking for speeders. Anne was stopped doing 23 mph over the limit and was looking at a very big fine. Worse, she was leaving the country soon to take Melissa home to Vietnam for a visit and would probably not make her court date.

Well, as luck would have it, she got Judge Daniel Sputnik, (not his real name) the only judge that I have ever met that was very Republican and very Gay. He always had the hots for me; I have no idea why as I am not terribly good looking, but I was smart, personable, and always "dressed to the nines" in court. At the traffic arraignment, the local prosecutor generally has the cases proceed to trial, because most lawyers wave this hearing, as you never get a case dismissed there. Otherwise, defendants show up without a lawyer and if they plead not guilty, they get their case assigned to a trial date.

That day, when my wife's case was called, Judge Sputnik said, with a beaming smile on his face,

'Mr. Pauly, it is wonderful to see you back in my courtroom today, how are you?

'Excellent your honor, how are you? I responded.

'Having a busy morning but,' he said with a laugh 'they are all busy. Is that a Hickey Freeman suit you are wearing?

'It is, your honor.

'And I know that beautiful tie that you are wearing is Ferragamo, but I don't recognize the pattern. Did you get it around here?

'No, your honor, my local tailor as wonderful as he is, only carries Robert Talbot instead of Ferragamo.

'Ah yes, Talbot, lovely English tie maker from Saville Row in London,' responded the judge, 'so where did you get your tie?

'From the Ferragamo store in Rome, your honor, just off the Via Condotti, sadly all of their suits were made for tall fit men like yourself, not lawyers like me, who are overweight.

'I would never call you overweight Mr. Pauly, "Meat and Potatoes" as they say perhaps, but not overweight. he giggled.

Now during this bizarre interlude, the prosecutor had been clearing her throat for her chance to speak, but Judge Sputnik simply ignored her and got down to business and asked,

'Who is this person, I am not even going to try and pronounce their last name, and are they here in the courtroom?

'That person is my wife, your honor, and she is presently in Vietnam with our daughter.

A large sigh from the bench, when the judge asked,

'I guess there is no way that you will ever join us on the other side of the fence, Mr. Pauly?'

'Sorry judge, as much as I would like to, I was born thoroughly hetero.'

'No, Mr. Pauly you are a Metrosexual, you have the good taste that comes from being one of us, while actually not being one of us. Let me guess, if this ticket goes forward, you will be sleeping on the couch for a week?

'Probably a month your honor, my wife has a bit of a temper. (Which is a complete fabrication by the way, but a little white lie can't hurt from time to time)

'Well then, I will consider this matter closed, you have a good day Mr. Pauly and do not be a stranger.

'Thank you, your honor.

As I turned to leave the prosecutor screeched out, 'But what about the ticket your honor?'

I turned to glance at her and took in the short hair, no makeup and the cheap man's suit she was wearing and smiled, as Judge Sputnik is one of many gay men who cannot stand gay women, particularly when they are rude and have no fashion sense.

The judge responded, 'The ticket has been addressed counselor, next case.' he said strongly as he winked at me. As I left the courtroom, I knew how lucky I was to have drawn him as my wife's judge. This was a rare event, but they do happen.

Let's assume that your lawyer does not have an excellent relationship with the judge and that you and your lawyer are treated like everyone else. Your traffic case will then go like this.

Most likely your speeding ticket was based upon the reading on the cop's radar gun. Your lawyer will first try to object to the admission of the speeding evidence, as the cop has not testified as to the calibration/accuracy of the radar gun. This works occasionally, but unless your lawyer has a scientific background, and can ask the right questions, it can be difficult to challenge the science of the radar gun. Instead, your lawyer will object that the officer's testimony about the radar gun is hearsay.

WHAT IS HEARSAY YOU ASK?

Hearsay literally is self-evident; the person making a statement in court about something that they heard another person say is usually inadmissible. This is because, no one has any idea if the other person's statement was true or untrue, and they are not present in the courtroom to be asked any questions. Now there are many different exceptions to the hearsay rule, but the one that pertains in your traffic ticket case is the "Government Record Exception." This means that if there are documents that are normally created by the government, such as publications on the government's website, pamphlets, and other routine documents, they are admissible in court. Here, the specific document that could get the radar gun evidence admitted is a calibration certificate that the officer may try and use to get your speed admitted into the trial.

If your lawyer is sharp, he or she can argue that the certificate was issued by someone else, usually a state laboratory technician. Since that person is part of the prosecutorial team, they should be there to testify in person that the radar gun was accurate. While this argument is technically true, most courts will not agree to drag someone down from the lab to testify that the gun was accurate. They will either allow the certificate into evidence over your defense lawyer's objection or occasionally reject the certificate and exclude the results from the radar gun from evidence.

So, if the cop can get the ticket into evidence, things are starting to look a bit grim; but you're not sunk yet. Your lawyer will cross-examine the cop to make sure that he actually got you in your car, rather than someone else's car. Trust me; it happens, especially with the older radar guns. The older guns have a very wide beam, sort of like a flashlight, and there are many different signals bouncing back from lots of different cars. The cop simply identifies the car that he thinks is going the fastest and attributes the radar gun's data to your speeding car.

Now, most of these radar guns have been retired and replaced with a new laser gun, that is very specific, and it's really hard to shake the cop's testimony about which car he picked up on his gun. Now, presuming that the laser results are solid, your lawyer has one of two different tactics at this point, really go after the cop's credibility, or show the court all of the good things that you were doing, instead of focusing on your speeding.

I know by personal experience over 25 years that really going after the cop, unless you know that you can shake their testimony, is a loser from the start. The facts of a speeding ticket are pretty straightforward, and unless you know that the cop has lied on the stand or been reprimanded for something by the department, this is all but fruitless.

So, the alternative way to proceed is for your lawyer to ask a series of questions about your driving and your vehicle. The cross-examination would go like this:

Q:*Officer was my client weaving?*

A: *No, he was not.*

Q.*Was he on his cell phone?*

A: *No, he was not.*

Q:*Was he able to produce a copy of his registration and proof of insurance?*

A:Yes, he did (this works if you actually had your shit together, otherwise your lawyer will not ask it.)

Q:Did my client stop as soon as your lights went on?

A:Yes, he did.

Q:When you made contact with him, was he polite?

A:Yes, he was. (refer to my comment about rudeness earlier in this chapter)

Q:So, except for speeding, his driving was fine, correct?

A:Yes, that is true.

Q: Now officer, is it possible that my client was not paying attention to his speed?

A:Yes, anything is possible.

Q: Was there anything that indicated to you that he was intentionally speeding, such as drag racing?

A:No.

Q:Was my client under the influence of any drugs or alcohol?

A:No. (If you were, you will read about Driving While Intoxicated a little further on in the series)

Q:So, the only thing that my client did that was wrong, was speed, correct?

A:Yes.

Now, what has this testimony done? It has forced the officer to admit, that except for speeding, your driving was perfectly fine, setting up your own testimony, called Direct Examination with a very easy set of questions. It usually goes like this, with your lawyer asking you questions in court:

Q:Mr. Smith, do you remember being stopped by this officer?

A:Yes.

Q:Were you in a real hurry that day?

A:No.

Q:So, you were not speeding intentionally?

A:No.

Q:Would you please tell the court what happened then?

A:I was not paying attention to my speed, and I will never do it again. I could have caused an accident and possibly hurt or killed someone. I am very sorry for speeding. This whole thing was my fault.

What the proceeding testimony does is explain to the judge that you were human like anyone else and that you were not trying to break the law; that your speeding was accidental. At this point, the Judge will ask if the cop has any questions for you, and the cop will say no.

WHY WILL THE COP SAY NO?

Because your testimony only went to your "State of Mind", you did not contest any of the facts that the officer testified to. "State of Mind" is literally that, what was your thinking process at the time that you committed the infraction? Since you are the only person who literally knows what you were thinking at the time, it's very difficult, without other evidence, to challenge this type of testimony.

Now, if you had a good reason for speeding, such as you were driving to a fire as I mentioned above, or you are a medical practitioner and you got called into work in an emergency, this will come out in your testimony and the judge will certainly take it into consideration.

The best example of this, in addition to the previous example where my client did not get stopped because he showed the cop his Fireman's helmet, was my veterinarian's ticket. Now Laura, as I will call her, has been my veterinarian for all of my shelter rescue dogs for over twenty years. She is a wonderful person who really is dedicated to the health of animals. She also has a lead foot and likes to roar around town. The last time that she got caught, she was pulled over by "Robocop" a very tall officer whose entire family takes law and order very seriously.

His sister was a criminal judge at Metropolitan Court in Albuquerque for ages, and she convicted each and every person that ever appeared in her courtroom, no matter how weak the facts were, or if they were actually innocent. Tragically, she is now Chief Justice for the New Mexico Supreme Court, so the rights of anyone, except for the usual Republican stalwarts, big companies, land developers, and other Republican politicians are currently taking a big hit on her watch, but that's not that relevant right now.

So back to Laura and her speeding ticket, she was doing 19 mph over the limit on her way into her clinic. Officer Steve Sakitume *(pronounced Sock It To Me)* could not care less that she had a medical emergency to take care of, and simply wrote her up for a ticket. Thankfully, we drew a rather interesting judge on her case; let's call him Fred "Friendly" Sentry. You can read much more about Friendly Fred in my memoir, "Expensive Janitor," Friendly Fred, as he is known was a former seminarian and had huge respect for authority as a result thereof.

BUT THIS DOES NOT SOUND GOOD, DAVID, I DON'T WANT A LAW AND ORDER JUDGE TO HEAR MY CASE, DO I?'

Normally you would be correct, but as a staunch Catholic, Fred had specific levels of right and wrong in his head. So speeding is wrong, but saving an animal's life is right. Additionally, staunch Catholics believe in a strong social hierarchy, (*as a Recovering Catholic I know this, you will just have to trust m*e) and those people, whose jobs are to save your life, or your soul, are at the top of the good list. Veterinarians, ironically, rank above most doctors because everyone knows that they make very little money, and are truly dedicated to helping innocent animals. The only medical doctor that ranks as the absolute best on the good list is a pediatric oncologist or a cancer doctor for kids. These people walk on water and everyone in society will cut them a lot of slack.

But now, the case is called, and I announce 'David Pauly for Dr. Laura.'

Friendly Fred says, 'Doctor? What kind of doctor are you?'

I answer for Laura, 'Judge she is a veterinarian, and was dashing into work to save a severely injured dog from dying.'

'Well, I suspect that Dr. Laura has a lot more valuable things to do than stand in my courtroom for a simple speeding ticket. The case is dismissed; you are free to go Doctor.'

Now Robocop could not believe this, as he didn't even get a chance to speak, but he knew as we all did that you never contested anything that Friendly Fred said or did, it just made things a lot worse. Now truthfully, Laura was just heading into the office for a normal day, but as she did not perjure herself (lie) to the court, she could not get in trouble. Also, as I was testifying, which is generally not allowed by the way, to the state of the facts of the case, I could always claim that I had misunderstood what Laura told me. Besides, as I mentioned above, certain types of people get treated differently than others, even if the facts are identical.

But, if you are an ordinary person, with an ordinary job, instead of putting out literal fires, or saving lives, particularly furry ones, the matter will proceed like this.

After the testimony is over, the judge will ask the cop if they have any closing statement, and they will say no. The judge will ask your lawyer if they have a statement, and your lawyer will say yes. Your lawyer will point out all the good things that you were doing while driving and that it was just a momentary lapse of focus that caused you to speed. So, at this point, the judge has heard that you were speeding, that you admitted to speeding and are very sorry for it. Nine times out of ten, the judge will give you a sentence that will keep this ticket off your record, especially if you have a clean driving history. Even if the judge imposes a sentence that shows up on your record, they very well may suspend the sentence for 90-180 days to give you a chance to show them that you have learned your lesson. At the end of the suspension period, if you have not reoffended, your lawyer will file a Motion for Dismissal, with an Affidavit from you that you have not been caught again. The judge will then grant the motion and your record is clear.

IF YOU GET CONVICTED, HOWEVER, AND THE TICKET WILL APPEAR ON YOUR RECORDS, YOU CAN ALWAYS APPEAL THE TRAFFIC TICKET TO A SUPERIOR COURT.

Since a traffic ticket does not rise to the level of a recorded hearing, you get a *trial de novo*, which means a new trial. Your lawyer will file the appropriate paperwork, and the whole process starts all over again. By this point, the cop has probably given up, and won't show up again. If they do, they will probably agree to some sort of a deal just to make you and your lawyer shut up. It's very rare to have a cop show up and testify determinedly against you unless you really pissed them off. And hey, convictions for traffic tickets do happen, even with a lawyer, but as I have said, with our help you have a 90% chance or better of getting off the ticket. It's just a question of how much money and time you are willing to invest in defending your ticket.

CHAPTER 2

CARELESS DRIVING

THE NEXT BATCHES of moving violations are a bit more serious than speeding or being on your cell phone. These charges are Careless Driving, Drag Racing, and Reckless Driving. All of these charges come with potential, or in the case of Reckless Driving, mandatory jail time, lots of points on your license and a heavy fine. First up is Careless Driving, where you were literally driving carelessly, or as the statute says "Operate(ing) a motor vehicle without due care for other vehicles or pedestrians." Careless driving can take many forms: excessive speeding, causing a car accident, driving too fast for conditions (it was a blizzard outside and you were driving aggressively), even running someone over and killing them. Careless Driving is worse than speeding, but it goes to negligence rather than intent. This means, that while you were driving like a moron, you were not trying to be an idiot, you just happened to be one at that moment.

A great example of this is when my client, Jonah Garcia, moved some of his furniture from one broken down apartment to another in his old beat up Ford Bronco. Jonah and his brother have been criminal clients forever, constantly doing stupid self-destructive things to make their lives miserable. Fortunately for them, their mother re-married a really nice man, who had a decent amount of money so that the Garcia kids can keep paying their legal bills.

So Jonah has a load of junk and furniture in his Bronco and is heading west on I-40 to move into some rat trap down in Los Lunas, a town just south of Albuquerque. It's a nice fall afternoon on Sunday, and there is not very much traffic on the road when Jonah is slowly about to overtake a group of motorcycle riders who are traveling in the far right lane. Motorcycle riding is huge in New Mexico, just think back to that 1970's classic "Easy Rider" and you will get the picture. Sadly, New Mexico has actually devolved, rather than evolved from the early '70s, but you can read about that in my memoirs as well.

As Jonah is about to pass the first of the motorcycle riders, his cell phone rings and he moves to pick it up from the center console. Jonah, as it turns out, has been up for 48 hours and can barely see straight. But he has to be out of his previous dump today, or the Sheriff will come at 9 am Monday morning and take away all of his crap, as he has been evicted. As Jonah tries to get his phone, he drops it, and as it falls to his right, he tries to grab it, inadvertently jerking his Bronco over into the right lane. Jonah hears a big thump and crashes, as he runs over something and brings his Bronco to a stop halfway off the shoulder and halfway into the dirt on the side of the freeway.

To both Jonah's horror and the motorcycle riders', Jonah has tragically just run over one of the group, and there are bits of motorcycle and person squashed all over the lane. The ambulance arrives and according to the riders, who are all one family, by the way, they keep waiting for the lights to go on and for their very injured relative to be taken straight away to the hospital. Sadly, shockingly, the lights do not go on, and the family slowly, terribly realizes that their relative did not make it into the ambulance alive.

The police arrived and did a very thorough accident investigation, getting Jonah to give, Breath, Blood and Urine samples at the local hospital. All of the tests came back negative, and Jonah was incredibly shaken by the event, simply repeating that he had reached for his cell phone and his Bronco had swerved. There were independent witnesses that confirmed that he was not speeding, weaving, or driving badly up until that terrible moment. So Jonah was charged with Careless Driving, as this was the strongest charge that could reasonably fit the facts.

Jonah retained me as his attorney, and normally, I would be able to get someone off a Careless Driving ticket without too much effort. This case was different as there was a fatality involved, and after a long and protracted legal process, I had to file a *de novo* appeal with the District Court to try and keep him out of jail. There was a tentative deal in place with the Judge Del Sanchez-Chavez-Carbajal-Blanco, where she would allow Jonah to plead No Contest and be placed on House Arrest instead of actual jail.

WHY NO CONTEST YOU ASK?

Because when there is an accident involved in your traffic ticket and you are the person at fault, the last thing you want to do is admit your guilt in criminal court, as this guilty plea will follow you straight into the civil court for the damage that you caused in the accident. Another reason is that if you read the fine print on your insurance policy if you admit to liability, they will fail to cover you with the insurance that you have paid for. This is because no insurance company is interested in paying claims for their insured drivers, they are much more interested in paying their executives tens of millions in annual bonuses, and rewarding their shareholders, but I will save my invective rant against insurance companies for another book in this series.

So, Jonah is getting the best option possible, house arrest, so that he can go to work and pay his bills, but otherwise, his ankle bracelet will let the police keep an eye on him when he is supposed to be home. We are all set up to proceed with this deal when the probation officer, assigned to Jonah, approaches and smells the stale alcohol on his breath. One of Jonah's pre-trial conditions was no booze or drugs. The probation officer asks that the judge orders Jonah to take a piss test, and the results come back. Jonah didn't hit a single one of the drugs that they tested him for; nope, he lit up all five indicators, Alcohol, Marijuana, Cocaine, Methamphetamine, and Heroin.

I was dumbfounded, what in the name of God was he thinking? The judge wasted no time in incarcerating Jonah immediately for 90 days, and there was absolutely nothing that I could do for him. When I asked him what happened, he said:

'I was sure I was going to jail anyway, so I partied hard last night.'

Shaking my head, I said, 'You should have had some faith in me, I have always kept you out of jail before.'

So, the previous story was both interesting, and informative, as it shows what happens to you when you graduate from simple traffic tickets, to crimes that carry jail time. While you are awaiting trial, your behavior becomes very important. If you commit a crime where you are charged with a misdemeanor like Jonah was, the original judge will set conditions of release that you have to abide by, the usual ones, are no booze or drugs, not leaving the county without permission from the court, and of course no further arrests or offenses.

I always tell my clients to behave themselves while they are waiting for their court date. Unfortunately, about fifteen percent of them do not and wind up rotting in jail until their trial date comes up. So, if I have not said it loud enough for you yet, **Listen to your Lawyer!!** You have already made a bad mistake to be facing jail time in the first place; do not compound that mistake with another bad decision. Wait until your first case is over, if you can manage it, before you insist on breaking the law again.

Now, in most situations, except in the very rare event when you have created human road-kill, by driving badly, I can get your Careless Driving ticket reduced to "Failure to Pay Attention", which carries two points instead of six, no jail time, and a minimal fine. If things go really well for you, and I can get the judge to agree to Defensive Driving School, you might avoid a conviction or fine altogether. One last remark, however: **Do not party the night before your trial!**, there are only so many miracles that we lawyers can pull off, and lighting up the Drug Dipstick, means that you are going "Straight to Jail", you will not "Pass Go", and you will not "Collect $200" to use the "Monopoly Game language."

CHAPTER 3
DRAG RACING

Now, we escalate from the extreme negligence of Careless Driving up to the next nasty traffic offense, Drag Racing. Drag Racing, unlike Careless Driving, is an intentional offense. This means, that you were actually speeding on purpose, racing your car against someone else. Instead of doing this on a race track, deserted airstrip, or some other reasonably safe place, you and your partner in crime do this in town on a Friday or Saturday night. Why do it where you could kill someone? Because your testosterone-addled twenty-something mind needs an audience to witness that your souped-up piece of shit '82 Chevy Nova is faster than your opponent's equally altered piece of shit '83 Ford Fiesta.

As you and your buddy are thinking of racing in NASCAR, the red light in front of you changes to green and with a squeal of tires, emitting a cloud of burning rubber, you blow past the speed limit of 40mph on your way to a hundred. Now, if by the grace of God, good luck and young reflexes, you don't cause a crash, you have gotten very lucky. But your antics have registered with the cops and one of them is in a high-speed pursuit of you. Now, you face an interesting choice, as there is only one cop car behind you and your friend, the one that they catch is the one that will get arrested, so to quote The Clash, *"Should I stay or should I go? If I stay there will be trouble and if I go there will be double."*

This lyric could not be more fitting, because if you pull over, you will get arrested for Drag Racing, but if you flee, you might still get caught, adding Evading and Eluding an officer, Careless or Reckless Driving to your list of charges, and potentially kill someone in the process. Or, as it happens quite often, the faster, better driver actually does escape arrest and makes it safely back home.

So, presuming that your car is too slow to avoid the cops, or you have a modicum of common sense remaining after deciding to drag race, you pull over and wait for the officer. This time, when the cop asks why you were driving so fast, you say," I don't know, I just felt like it."

BUT WAIT A MINUTE; DIDN'T YOU SAY EARLIER THAT BEING HONEST WITH THE COP IS INCREDIBLY IMPORTANT?

Yes, I did, but not when you are facing criminal charges. As a soon-to-be Defendant, **you don't lie to the police ever**, **but you don't tell them everything**. After all, you did "just feel like" speeding, but as the cop has not caught your buddy, all they can do is assume that you were intentionally Drag Racing. If you admit it to the cop, it will make my job a lot harder at trial.

When we go to court on your case, we might be able to work out a deal with the cop to send you to Defensive Driving school, get the Drag Racing dropped to Careless Driving, or if I am having a really great day in court, to a high range speeding ticket.

BUT YOU JUST TOLD ME ABOUT CARELESS DRIVING AND HOW IT CAN CARRY JAIL TIME, WHY IS THIS ANY GOOD?

Because while Careless Driving carries the "possibility" of jail time and 6 points on your license, Drag Racing carries a "mandatory" five days in jail, and ten out of ten points on your license, which will suspend your license for a year. Drag Racing is really stupid and really dangerous, so if you have to do it, choose some deserted road in the desert, or better yet, an old runway near a deserted airfield.

One of my more clever examples in successfully beating a Drag Racing charge involved my client Johnny Nguyen. Johnny, as you can guess from his last name, is Vietnamese, and Vietnamese males in Albuquerque, have for the most part a massive inferiority complex, as they are shorter than the Hispanics, Native Americans, or White people, and are just starting out on the typical destructive pathway that most young men in New Mexico embark upon. So, Johnny is racing his cousin Tommy Pham, but Johnny is the one that gets caught.

When I have Johnny bring in his driving history from Motor Vehicles, I can see that he is down to the last two points on his license and that he has had over a half-dozen moving violations in his short 5-year driving career. The judge, no matter who it is, is going to throw the book at him, and he very well might be doing more than five days in jail, and the judge might even try to confiscate his car. This is because he and his cousin chose to drag race down the middle of Montgomery Avenue, starting at the Eubank intersection. Not only is this ground zero for Drag Racing in Albuquerque, but it is also always monitored on Friday and Saturday nights. Johnny and his cousin tore off down the street when it was quite crowded and amazingly did not hit anyone or anything.

So, after I gave Johnny and his mother the sad news, I came up with a radical suggestion.

'Johnny, I need you to sell your car, so that I can show the judge that you literally can't do this again.

'No way man, I love my car.

'I know, but if you don't listen to me, you are going to jail, you will lose your license for a full year, and the judge might confiscate your car and then where will you be? Do you have a friend, preferably an older female that you can sell the car to for a while?

'What do you mean a "while"?

'What I am planning is to show the judge that you did indeed sell your car and that you are no longer a threat to the community. Furthermore, I want to bring in the new owner, who hopefully is old and female, and really unlikely to drag race, to convince the judge to let you off. After the court date is over, you can buy the car back from the new owner, a deal that you two will work out ahead of time. There is very little chance of this failing to work, especially if the woman is not a relative. What do you think?

Johnny thought for a bit, smiling the whole time; because he loved my devious plan and he was smart enough to know this time he was in trouble. So he agreed to do it.

On the day of trial, I met Johnny, his mom, who was paying my fee by the way, and an older Hispanic woman, Victoria Sanchez. It turns out that Ms. Sanchez was the mother of Johnny's ex-girlfriend, of whom he had fathered a child. Johnny did have some sense of responsibility and paid his child support on time, so he was amazingly still a friend of the family, so they had cooked up a deal, that "officially" I was not aware of, concerning the car. Most importantly, Johnny and Ms. Sanchez could truthfully say that they were not blood relatives and that she had seen an ad in the "Quick-Quarter" newspaper, which I had Johnny place for 2 weeks running prior to his trial.

Thankfully, we had drawn Judge Rivera-Chavez as the judge on this case, a real indecisive idiot from a politically well-connected family. I spend some time talking about him in my memoirs, but all you need to know is what I just told you, and as a politician, he wants to please everyone. So, when we get into court, I first have to take a crack at the officer.

Thankfully, I know Officer Johnson from several other cases, and I ask him to reduce the Drag Racing to Careless Driving, with a suspended sentence if Johnny goes to Aggressive Drivers School, a week-long set of classes designed exactly for people like Johnny. The course includes listening to the victims of insanely bad driving, or the families of people who have been severely injured, or killed by Drag Racers or

Reckless Drivers." Surprisingly, it has a very good track record, and usually, the people who attend do not re-offend.

Officer Johnson shakes his head and says, 'No David, I have seen this guy's car a bunch of times out on Montgomery, this is the first time that I could catch him. He was driving a "Rice Rocket" (Cop slang for a souped-up car driven by an Asian) and I know that he will do it again.

'Officer, he actually sold the car to someone who is not related to him, he no longer owns a car.'

Now Officer Johnson as a good cop is naturally paranoid and suspicious, so he asks, 'You don't expect me to take your word for it, do you?'

'No Officer, the woman who bought the car from my client is here in court and will swear under oath, that she is not related to my genius client, that she will not let him borrow the car, and she has brought proof of the transfer of title with her. How about it?

Officer Johnson could not think of any objection, so he agreed to a plea to high range speeding ticket with a deferred sentence on condition of attending, Aggressive Driving School, a three-hundred-dollar contribution to crime stoppers, and on condition of no further incidents.

When we brought this up in front of the Judge, he was a bit suspicious, but after Ms. Sanchez, a matronly 53-year-old grandmother, and clearly Hispanic, not Asian, showed him the transfer of title, he grudgingly went along with the deal. As we walked out of court, I told Johnny, 'This is the last miracle that I can do for you. If you get caught again for any tickets in the next 2 years, your license is gone, and you are probably going to go to jail, got it?

'Yes,' said Johnny, 'So long as I get my car back.'

Ms. Sanchez said to Johnny, 'I worked out a deal with your mom, you can buy the car back after you complete your classes, repay your mom all of your lawyer fees, and don't do anything stupid for 3 months got it?

Johnny started to whine and argue, so I excused myself as quickly as possible and left the building. So to reiterate, if you get caught for Drag Racing, be prepared to pay the consequences, as they will be more severe than a simple traffic ticket. Your lawyer will hopefully come up with a way to limit the damage but remember you were the one who chose to do the crime, it wasn't negligence this time, it was intentional willful stupidity.

CHAPTER 4
RECKLESS DRIVING

Reckless Driving is right up at the top of the ladder for moving violations that do not involve a DWI; the other offense is "Eluding or Evading a Police Officer."

Reckless Driving is a self-defined offense, which states "The operator of a motor vehicle drove recklessly, endangering others." While there may be an intentional component to this crime, the charge usually comes from really bad driving and often accompanies other offenses, such as DWI, Vehicular Homicide, but it can be a charge on its own. Reckless Driving carries a mandatory 5 days in jail; along with a full year of suspension of your driving privileges.

A good example of this that does not involve another crime would be speeding through a school zone, or speeding way above the limit. Now, as you will find out later, I do not help anyone who hurts other people, it's my moral line in the sand. Speeding through a school zone, particularly an elementary school puts little kids at risk, so no way am I going to help. However, here is a classic example of someone driving recklessly without injuring anyone.

Mr. Walker and his friend, Mr. Jones were being inducted into the United States Air Force the following Monday. So, naturally, they

DO I NEED A LAWYER?   31

wanted to go out and have one last fun evening before reporting to boot camp. They both got on their motorcycles and headed east on Paseo del Norte, a small highway between the suburb of Rio Rancho and Albuquerque. They had been up all night playing video games, relying on Jolt Cola to keep them awake. They got the bright idea, that they would have one last spin on their motorcycles, so at 3 am, they tore through the deserted suburban streets in Rio Rancho and really hit the gas once they got onto Paseo del Norte. There was a cop at the 4th street intersection, which saw them blow by, and as he got in hot pursuit, he realized that he was doing 150 mph, and was barely keeping up with them. The two geniuses were having such a good time that they were oblivious to the cop behind them. Amazingly they screeched to a halt at the red light at the I-25 intersection waiting for it to turn green, so they could continue their madcap journey. A minute or so later, they saw the flashers and realized that they were in big trouble.

When they both came to my office, I saw that the criminal complaint charged them with Reckless Driving and an estimated speed of 155mph when they passed the cop. When I asked them the usual "what happened" and "why" questions, their response was simple and believable, they were out for one last fun night before joining up. Their Motor Vehicle Department (MVD) records were both clean, so these guys had just made one giant mistake.

Their bikes had been impounded by the police and were released to them the following day. Their fathers, both military veterans themselves, flat out ordered their sons to sell the bikes, which the boys did.

So, when the day of trial came around, the officer was adamant about a conviction for both of them. Even the presence of their recruiting officer from the Air Force could not change the officer's mind.

As they did not have a valid excuse, all I could do was have them plead no contest to the charge and hope that their judge, Sandy Nixon, would not whack them too hard. What I knew, but the cop did not know, was that Sandy's husband was a District Court judge, and loved his Harley. He rode it every day unless it was raining to the courthouse, and I knew that Sandy loved to be on the back of his bike. So, this was my tiny little edge, going in.

Once the case was called, I had my clients change their plea of not guilty to no contest. The judge let the cop rant for a couple of minutes about how these guys were trying to imitate a Cruise Missile, before asking me for my thoughts on a sentencing recommendation.

I was able to hand her endorsed copies of the MVD records from both clients, the sale paperwork for both motorcycles, and state that the recruiting sergeant from the Air Force was here, and that they would be inducted today, if they were allowed to remain out of jail and did not have a criminal conviction on their record.

This was a tough decision for Sandy, as their behavior warranted a conviction, but they were on their way to serve their country. Sandy talked briefly and sternly to both men, and then imposed a charitable contribution of $300.00 and agreed to a 180-day defense continuance. The cop was nearly apoplectic at this point, but when the recruiting sergeant spoke up, that the boys were headed out of town to Lackland Air force Base in San Antonio, Texas, he knew how hot it was, as this was July, and began to calm down. Once the cop was told that the boys would spend 7 grueling weeks in boot camp, before heading out to technical training at Sanford Air force Base, for another 3 months, and then be deployed overseas, he was ok with the sentence.

At no time in the foreseeable future would the boys be in the State of New Mexico, and they would understand the meaning of discipline and responsibility by the time that they were deployed. This was enough to calm the officer down, but ironically if the boys had simply been local kids, they would have been convicted of a more serious offense, and would certainly have gotten community service, loss of their license for a year, and possibly jail time as a result of their conviction.

Now, unless you really feel the need to drive like a maniac, with a high probability of dying, killing someone else, or both, **do not drive reck-**

lessly, there will not be a good outcome for you, no matter how brilliant your lawyer is, unless the officer fails to appear in court. The last of the traffic offenses that we are covering in this book is "Evading or Eluding an Officer."

CHAPTER 5

EVADING AND OR ELUDING AND OFFICER

Here we are at the last moving violation related matter that you are likely to face, unless and until you decide to start drinking and driving. Evading or Eluding an officer is just what it sounds like when the flashers go on behind you and you fail to pull over immediately. When I am talking about immediately, I mean in a minute or so, or as soon as you notice that there are red and blue lights coming up behind you at a high rate of speed.

WHY DO PEOPLE EVADE OR ELUDE YOU ASK?

That's a good question; one usually based upon the fact that the driver doesn't want to get arrested for another perhaps more serious crime. For example, if you have the body of someone that owes you money in the trunk of your car, and you see the lights behind, you will probably panic and take off. After all, unless you are the two hardened criminals from "Pulp Fiction" who have a mobster fix it man, nicknamed "The Wolf" available to help them dispose of an unexpected body, you will probably panic worse than they did.

Most people, who get busted for Evading and Eluding, are usually the slower person in a drag race, which you read about in the previous chapter, and it's a completely subjective crime. In other words, there is no objective test about the crime; you can be an extremely elderly driver, for example, blind as a bat, and completely oblivious to the fact that an officer wants you to stop. Usually, my clients that have been charged with this have sped up and tried to lose the cop, which by the way, unless you are literally driving a Ferrari with the lights off, is probably not going to happen. Now, if you have a motorcycle, and really know how to ride it, you can probably lose a cop by hitting 3 sharp turns around suburban blocks, that the cop can't navigate as quickly. I had a fraternity brother in college who pulled that off a couple of times, so it can be done, but you are talking about hitting a corner in a quiet neighborhood at 70 mph or greater. Presuming that you don't become an organ donor from your act of moronic bravado, you very well may escape.

One thing that a fleeing driver never realizes is that radio signals travel at the speed of light, and the cop will alert other cops that he is chasing some dangerous knucklehead down the road. Again, if you are an F1 driver in one of your race cars, you have a chance to get away, with an even better chance of ending up as the liquid contents of a car that now resembles an accordion.

When you finally stop and face the inevitable music, you are going to be dealing with one angry cop. Not only were you a greater menace to society than his normal traffic stop, but you were also flouting his authority by not stopping quickly enough. Most cops have a real macho attitude, especially the female ones, so they took the job in the first place either to do societal good or to become a poor imitation of James Bond. While they do not wear a seven-thousand-dollar tux, custom made by Ralph Lauren, they do have a tailored polyester suit, a weapons belt rather than a gadget kit, and an American-made car which is faster than most of the sports cars out there. They may not be chasing Blofeld from SPECTRE, but chasing your dumb ass is as close as they are going to get to it in this lifetime. Trust me when I say this, as much as they don't want to see someone eluding and evading them, it's what really gets their adrenaline flowing, and they can feel albeit briefly, that their life and job are cooler than they actually are.

As the officer approaches your window, your best defense is to say the following, "Sorry officer, I did not see you back there, I was not paying attention." Now inattentive driving is an admission to the offense of the same name, but it does not carry mandatory jail time, nor is it an automatic suspension of your license for a year. While you know it's bullshit, and so does the cop, it gives the cop another ticket to write, and gives us lawyers an option to have you plea to this charge in court, rather than the nastier Evading or Eluding.

Unless the cop is more gullible than usual, he will not believe you for a second, so being humble and apologetic is the best way to go, as I have said many times in this book so far. If you let the cop re-establish their authority and acknowledge that they are in control, you are halfway to having me get a decent deal in court. If you start arguing, or worse, "Lawyering" the cop, you are hosed, and all I will be able to do is throw your ass on the mercy of whichever courtroom we wind up in.

Prepare to be arrested if you Evade and Elude; just like if you are driving on a Suspended or Revoked driver's license. We will cover both of these separate crimes in the second book of this series, as they are usually, but not always related to Driving While Intoxicated by something. You had better hope as the handcuffs are being snapped on to your wrists, that there is nothing worse than a McDonalds' wrapper and loose change in your car. By committing an arrestable offense, the officer can, and will, do an inventory search of your vehicle. So long as the cop does not think that drugs or other serious crimes are involved, he will probably not search your spare tire wheel well or go through all of the crap in your trunk.

Once you get bailed out of jail, contact a traffic lawyer immediately, this charge carries a full suspension of your license for a year, and mandatory jail time, along with the most expensive fine that is allowable under State Law for a Misdemeanor. Plus, you can forget about your insurance, you will have to find some company dumb enough and sleazy enough, like the ones I mentioned earlier in the book to insure your dumb ass.

Your lawyer will go through most of the steps necessary to try and get you out of this ticket and salvage your driver's license. However, this time, no matter how hard your lawyer works, if you have a bad driving history, or you really pissed off the cop, you will probably get convicted.

BUT WHY?

Because, everyone in the criminal justice system, wants people to obey the cops when the flashers go on behind them. Simply not paying attention for a minute or so will not get you arrested for this charge, you really do have to earn it. Why does the system take this so seriously? The most obvious reason is that if you are Evading and Eluding, you are probably driving like a bat out of hell, very likely to kill yourself or some innocent person.

Once the officer testifies that he or she activated their emergency flashers when they were behind you, and you failed to stop, it's not a good look for you. When they continue and say that you sped up, changed lanes frequently, exited or entered the freeway, or whipped around corners trying to lose them, your only hope is one of two things. The first is that your lawyer will cross-examine the cop to make certain that they did not lose sight of you in their pursuit. Trust me this happens from time to time.

One of my clients that you will read about in my Driving While Intoxicated book had the bad misfortune of blowing through a suburban intersection, slamming on their brakes and nearly T-boning a police car. The police car was able to get my client's license plate number but my client simply screamed out of the intersection back the way that the cop came from, and actually got away from the cop. Bad news for the client was that he parked his truck in his own driveway, and when the cops arrived 3 minutes later, they found that the engine hood was hot. They went around the side of his house, and genius was pretending to be asleep on his couch, but forgot to pull the curtains across the sliding back door, and forgot to lock the door. Needless to say, they identified him, entered the house on the pretext of checking on my client's safety, and arrested him for DWI. At trial, I tried to argue that while the cop may have seen my client's vehicle, they did not see his face, so there was no proof that he was driving the vehicle. Unfortunately, for my client, he had a very recognizable haircut and mustache, just like Sonny Bono used to have in the 1970s. I had tried to get my client to get a crew cut, and shave off his facial hair so that identity would be more difficult, but sadly, like many of my clients, he failed to listen to me. Needless to say, he was convicted.

While it's possible that the officer may have lost sight of your vehicle for a few minutes if they got your license plate number, they will find your vehicle for sure. So, if you lose the cops, park your vehicle as soon as possible, and not in your own driveway, and get away from your car as soon as possible. Now if the cops see someone walking away from your vehicle, they will stop that person, so the faster you can put some distance from your car the better. Crossing the street to change directions is good while getting around a corner of a block is even better. Most likely, however, you will not be able to lose them. At that point, you are at the mercy of the judge, which is never a good look for you. But, if you follow the script that I wrote for you in terms of apologizing, admitting that you were not paying attention, and sticking with this story, we very well may be able to convince a judge that you were not intentionally driving like an asshole.

CHAPTER 6
SOLICITATION OF A PROSTITUTE

Right, well this is one of my favorite cases when I represent someone, as the client is nearly always a male that asked a question that he should not have.

WHY THE MAN AND NOT THE WOMAN?

Because while prostitutes get caught themselves, the usual procedure is to target their customers or "Johns" as the Sidewalk Stewardesses call them, for reasons I can only guess. It's probably, because while men might learn their lesson on breaking the law, the women for reasons that are nearly always very unfortunate, are unable to.

WHY IS THIS MY FAVORITE TYPE OF CASE?

Because unlike nearly every other type of case; I usually have complete client control. The clients are terrified that their family, boss, or church will find out that they were trying to get laid with a streetwalker.

These guys routinely set up a post office box so that their court notices and correspondence from my office will go there instead of home.

Better yet, they pay in cash, as they certainly do not want their wives to see a credit card charge to a lawyer, and ask what it is about. The only difficult time is when the men come into the office with their wife, who found out somehow that they got arrested for solicitation, but thankfully that is relatively rare.

Prostitution is called the world's "Oldest Profession", and it probably is, with loan sharks and lawyers not being too far behind. Why is prostitution illegal you ask? There are two sides to this question, one of which comes from a health and welfare standpoint, which is difficult to refute, and the other is combined with the persistent rise of angry feminism.

The first reason is that the sexual exploitation of women, kids, and even men, is morally reprehensible, no one should be forced to do anything that they do not want to do, particularly of a sexual nature. Force can be direct, such as your parent is a drug addict and pimps you out to supply their habit, or indirect, where the prostitute is addicted to drugs, or is so poor, that they have no other way to survive. The other part of this argument is the presence of sexually transmitted diseases, (STD) that keep getting ahead of medical treatments to treat them or prevent them. AIDS, Hepatitis C, Methicillin-Resistant Staphylococcus Aurous (MRSA) resistant bacteria, are all diseases that are preventable from being transferred from one person to the next.

The second reason is as I said is the rise of angry feminism, that insistence on a monogamous relationship between men and women. Men, historically, were more prone to seek out a prostitute for the simple reason that if they caused a pregnancy, the man was not forced to carry the child. So, to a large degree, men could run around and do what they wanted to do with few repercussions. Women, on the other hand, were and still are the only half of our species that can conceive, and until very recently in a historical sense, they were stuck with the child, barring a convenient miscarriage.

BUT WHY ANGRY FEMINISM YOU ASK?

Because women in the late 19th and early 20th century were sick and tired of their men both getting drunk and having sex with another woman. This was not just an emotional construct as women had a right to be concerned about the transmission of STD's to themselves. Overall, however, the Victorian societal model did not tolerate "Vices" as they were known historically, and this attitude peaked around 1920. The "Mann Act" (yes its actually called that, no matter how funny it is), which prohibited the interstate transportation of sex workers, was passed in 1910, and by the outbreak of the first world war, nearly every state in the United States had passed laws prohibiting prostitution.

It took the feminists another 9 years before they were allowed to vote, and it took them less than one more year to prohibit the sale of alcohol. Now, the angry feminists were happy, as their men could no longer drink, party with hookers, and had to stay home at night. So long as their men were miserable and bored, they were forced to listen to their wives, which of course drove them to seek out illicit sources of entertainment. So, after the wife fell asleep, thinking that she had finally gotten her "Man" to "listen" to her at last, the husband, who was contemplating suicide, while listening to the same boring tirade he had been listening to for years, snuck out of the house, looking to get drunk and laid.

Sadly, all this did in both cases was push drinking and prostitution underground, leading to the rise of organized crime, as portrayed in many different gangster movies set in the "Roaring Twenties". While well intentioned, prohibiting human behavior by law is a delicate balancing act between too much or too little regulation with a corresponding restriction or lack of it for personal freedom. Even in countries like Saudi Arabia, where alcohol and prostitution are illegal, it still goes on; the penalties are just much more severe. So today, depending on the country, the state, or even the city, prostitution still flourishes.

Ok enough of the history lesson, but it's important to look at the legal system in context sometimes. After all, before 1900, the automobile was not available, so there were no laws necessary to regulate how you drove a car. Other crimes have been around for a much longer time.

Now, to a practical example of this crime; it's a hot summer night, and in nearly every town, and certainly every city in the US, there are sex workers out there earning a living. So, let's take "Jim's" case as an example. Jim is in his mid 30's to mid 40's married, and white, with a couple of kids. Nonetheless, he is out driving down Central Avenue in Albuquerque looking for a good time. Why, do you ask? Because, and I quote one of the infamous prostitutes from the only legal brothel in the United States, The Bunny Ranch, when she says, *"I do the things that wives are not comfortable doing."* A better summation for a prostitute's purpose is hard to find.

What "things", do you ask? Well, we can start with different sexual positions, go through blow jobs, and take a brief stop in Bondage Land, before culminating in anal sex, threesomes, and even more interesting/bizarre behavior, involving costumes and even livestock. As I used to tell the wives who found out that their husbands had been arrested for prostitution, "If they can't get what they want at home, they will go get take out." While this generally infuriated the wives, it was and is actually true. Every one of my male clients that was arrested fits the profile in the above paragraph.

These were happily married men, who were bored with their sex life and wanted something different. None of them wanted a divorce, or even a steady girlfriend on the side, they just wanted a different flavor of their favorite thing, sex. Everyone and I mean every one of my male "johns" who got busted over the years always wanted a blow job, except for the one guy who wanted to start with oral pleasure and then finish in her butt. And none of them could get a blow job from the wife at home, much less a little back door adventure.

While I am not pointing fingers here, as a male, I can understand my client's desire, and cannot understand for the life of me why women will not give their men a blow job. I mean it's not as if it is unhygienic, immoral, or illegal, it just boggles my mind. Plus, a concurrent complaint from many married women is that they don't get an orgasm from the 2 to 4 minutes that their men last in the Missionary Position. So, if the husband goes down on the wife and does it properly, she will squirt and squeal, and want sex more often, and will have no moral authority to deny the husband what he wants. But as this would make sense, where marital sex is concerned, the concept is doomed to failure.

On a "Good for Society" note, having better sex at home would reduce the need for take-out. It would reduce prostitution by well over half if not more, but for various cultural, religious, and feminist reasons, getting a first-class blow job at home has always been hard to come by (pun intended) and is becoming ever more difficult.

So, Jim slows down where the hookers are standing and waits until a reasonably attractive woman approaches his car and she asks, "Hey, looking for a date?" Jim says "Yes, how much for a Blow Job?" She says $20 and if Jim is lucky, they pull around the corner and 5-10 minutes later, the hooker is $20 richer and Jim is on his way home, to have a shower before climbing into bed with his wife. If Jim is not so lucky, the attractive woman is the only attractive one wandering around, and as soon as he asks how much for a Blow Job, she flashes her badge, and tells him to pull over and park for his arrest.

WHY DOESN'T JIM TAKE OFF AT THIS POINT?

Because, the cops have his plate number already, and in one of these stings there is always a cop ready to pursue anyone who tries to flee.

NOW, WHAT ABOUT ENTRAPMENT, MY FRIEND THAT GOT BUSTED SAID IT WAS ENTRAPMENT?

Entrapment is very difficult to prove, particularly if the undercover cop is not using a tape recording as evidence, but simply testifies in court. There is no way she will make any statement that brings entrapment to mind in court.

BUT WHAT IS ENTRAPMENT YOU ASK?

Entrapment, without the complex legal window dressing, is when a police officer encourages you, if not actually causes you to commit a crime. A good example would be a cop trying to increase his Drunk Driving arrests, and buying people shots in a bar He would encourage the drunk to get into their car, and as soon as they pull out on to the street, he will radio his partner to pull the drunk over. Now, I have never seen this happen before, but there are clients of mine who think that they were "Entrapped" into soliciting a hooker.

An Entrapment would go like this. Jim rolls the window down on his car, and the woman approaches and says "would you like a date tonight?" Jim says "Sure, hop in." Now, Jim has not yet committed a crime, in fact, no one has. There are no laws against meeting someone in public and wanting to have sex with them. Just think of every airport or singles bars that you have been in, lots of people are willingly hooking up without breaking the law.

Back to Jim, who says, 'Hey, my wife is out of town, do you want to go back to my place?' The woman says, 'No, let's just have sex here.' Jim goes around the corner to park his car. Again, without paying or offering to pay for the sex, no crime has been committed, unless Jim gets caught by a cop walking by and is cited for indecent exposure. But if Jim asks, 'How much will this cost me?', he is screwed, in all the ways but the one that he actually wanted if he is propositioning an undercover cop. But, if the female undercover cop says "Hey, a Blow Job is $20, would you like one?" and Jim agrees, that is called Entrapment. Up until the point where money is mentioned no crime has been committed, and Jim can't be arrested for anything. If the undercover cop asks him for money first, the argument is that he would not have broken the law without her initiating the crime.

Now, this rarely happens, as most guys are too stupid and too impatient to be subtle, and also, nine times out of ten, the wife is only out of the house for a couple of hours and they need to make their "sexcapade" as short as possible so that they do not get caught. So, after their arrest, this is when they come to my office. All they want to do is make it go away, they do not want to go to court, certainly do not want a trial and would find testifying mortifying. Worse, there is usually a person from Mothers Against Drunk Driving "MADD" who is taking notes on how many drunk driving cases get tossed out of the courtroom. They write these statistics down so that the public can keep track of a judge's law enforcement record. They also keep statistics on lots of things and have no compunction of taking notes in court and bandying the stories around town. So, the more often Jim goes to court, the more likely that he will be revealed as a "Whoremonger" to use an archaic expression.

When we go to court, if the undercover cop is there, I cut a deal with her on the best terms that I can get. As Solicitation is a petty misdemeanor, the lowest level of crime, there is no mandatory jail time or community service involvement. Once the deal is struck, Jim can go on with his life, hoping that his wife never decides to look him up on the Court website, as all criminal offenses, even those that are dismissed remain public record forever.

In conclusion, guys, and I am speaking to both men and women here, going out to find a hooker on the street is a really bad idea; it's where nearly all arrests happen. If you try to talk your partner into being less boring in the bedroom and fail, you can always try counseling. This is a tough one because if he/she feels that your needs are immoral, or just plain gross, you are back to square one. So if you need to find someone else to play with, contact one of the escort services in the classified section of a newspaper, and do it from your hotel room, **do not call on your cell phone**! This way, unless you are incredibly unlucky, you will get what you want from someone much more expensive, and much better looking than the streetwalker with the missing teeth.

Also, always pay cash for the room and the fun, and if you are reasonably clever to take out small amounts on a semi-regular basis, so that once per month there isn't a $500.00 withdrawal from your joint checking account that pops out at your partner when they are reviewing your finances. Now, if you are into getting "take out" on a regular basis, try and have your paycheck split into two amounts, or use rental or investment income or some other stream of money which is deposited into a different bank than the one that you have your regular accounts with.

Also, get the P.O. Box set up as well, so that the one day that your partner gets to the mail first, he/she does not see that you have a secret stash of cash. The more careful you are, the less likely you will need to come to see me for this. Additionally, once you start enjoying your expensive "takeout" do not alter your routine at home. If your partner is used to having sex once or twice a month, like most married white couples, make sure that you do not alter your plans. Do the partner when and how they want, and then get takeout another night. If you slowly reduce your complaining that you are not getting oral pleasure, or locked up in handcuffs, rather than stop suddenly, your partner will simply think that you have come to your senses. Patterns are the way that criminals get caught, so change the night that you get take out, and the time, do not have a regular night away from home unless you have a great reason for being out of the house. The last thing you need to worry about is coming up with an excuse, or a believable answer to your partner's angry question with a straight face at 1 am "Where have you been?"

The reason for a regular absence at night is not that difficult to create, but it has to be something where your partner has no interest in going along with you, and something that they believe you might do. Examples of good excuses for absences are some of the following weekly or monthly meetings for Car Restoration, Fly Fishing, Welding Classes at the local community college, a Poker game (this explains the cash withdrawals by the way), or if your more nerdy, an Electronics club, Chess club, Auditioning new audio gear, that sort of thing. Do not try something stupid like a book club, poetry club, dance lessons, or anything that is not believable, or worse, something that your partner might try and gate crash. Make sure, that there is actually a meeting of your group or club so that if your partner gets nosey, and decides to follow up on the meeting, he/she can see that it is real on the internet, or even in person if necessary. Now, if you are enjoying a convenient sheet shuffle at the hotel when he/she decides to drop in on your fly-fishing meeting, you are out of luck. All you can do is think on the spot, but you will probably get caught.

Now, the next clever bit of infidelity and this is much more likely with a regular girlfriend/boyfriend, than an escort, is to make certain that there is no evidence of your transgressions. This means, no perfume/cologne odors, no visible stains on your clothing from lipstick, makeup or bodily fluids, no strands of hair that do not belong to you or your partner, and last but not least, no visible marks on your body, particularly scratch marks or hickeys. This means that if you are seeing a dominator or dominatrix, for example, you need to get the padded handcuffs and instruct her to discipline you in ways that will not leave whip marks on your ass.

Now the prior examples require forethought and proper planning, but if you have had the hots for someone at work for a while, and at the company mixer, you really hit it off with them, you can bet that there is no plan whatsoever. At least get the proverbial room, preferably with cash, or their credit card, and after the fun is over, take a shower, to remove perfume or cologne from your body, along with any makeup. If there is no shower, or you forget to take one, stop off at a gas station and spill a little gas on your clothes. Trust me, gasoline is one of the strongest and most recognizable odors out there and it will cover nearly anything else. But using the gas ploy only cover up odors, if there is lipstick on your collar, bite marks on your neck or a fake fingernail that winds up in your clothes and it is found, you will be reading my upcoming book on Divorce and Family Law.

Finally, choosing your playmate is a very important thing to do. If you are in a large enough city where the escort services are discreet and reliable, you should always stay with the same person. Much less risk of STD's, and much less risk of them tying you up on the bed, and extorting money as they are taking pictures of you with their phone.

The safest and probably the most enjoyable way to play with someone else works if you have a substantial amount of free cash. You can look up one of the Sugar Baby websites where the nubile pretty young thing is not actually a prostitute but wants a lifestyle that he/she cannot yet afford. All communication either goes through your work computer or a 2nd cell phone that your partner does not know about. Here, as always, discretion is key to not getting caught and subsequently divorced.

CHAPTER 7
POT POSSESSION

THIS CRIME IS FAIRLY straight forward if you, the client, are sensible and just want it to go away. However, if you are not sensible, and insist on a trial, then your case will get very expensive very quickly, and the odds of winning your case are not great. But you have the right to a trial under the law; it's just your choice. Now, the easy way to get rid of this is to have your lawyer make a deal for you that will keep this crime off your record. In states where there is a lot of pot smoking occurring, and trust me you can smell the odor of burning Oregano all over the place in New Mexico, getting a deal is relatively easy. However, if you are in a region with lots of "Severe Christians", you might have a harder time of it.

WHAT IS A "SEVERE CHRISTIAN", YOU ASK?

Someone that takes the Bible literally, every word, comma, and conjunction is the true word of God. They treat it like a cookbook, and all the answers to all of life's problems and questions are in there somewhere, if you just look hard enough. These people also think that the "Flintstones" is a documentary.

The problem with the Severe Christians is the association between two completely different concepts, Illegality, and Immorality. Most of them think that there is a direct linkage, that one word is defined by another. In referring back to the chapter about prostitution, most people, but especially the Severe Christians think that breaking the Sixth Commandment is immoral, that you are not supposed to "covet another man's wife". Now if you take this literally, it seems to only pertain to a married woman, it does not say anything about single people, gays, or anyone else. You can read about my questioning the literal interpretation of the Bible in my novel "Expensive Janitor: Spit Shine and Polish" where after much persuasion by my ex-wife, I attended a Sunday service at the First Baptist Church, where after a brief participation in discussing the Bible, I was asked to leave; Permanently.

Now, if your lawyer knows the judge's personal habits, which probably involves the consumption of some mind/mood altering substance, such as alcohol, pot, cocaine, etc. you are probably in good shape. But if not, and a deal is not available, then to trial, you will go. The steps that your lawyer will take are multilevel and time-consuming, thus the higher fee.

THE FIRST QUESTION IS: WHY DID THE COP INVESTIGATE YOU FOR POT IN THE FIRST PLACE?

Now, if you were foolish enough to smoke it in public in plain sight, and the cop walks by, this establishes the first hurdle that the prosecution has to overcome, a term called "Reasonable Suspicion." Reasonable Suspicion means exactly what it sounds like, would a "reasonable person" suspect that a crime might be going on. This is a very low threshold, an odor of pot, which for those of you that do not know is quite distinctive, is more than enough for a cop to make contact with you. Once this starts, your odds are going south in a hurry, he will search you, find the pot and then he will have what is called "Probable Cause" to make an arrest. Probable Cause is literally defined as "on the balance of probabilities, was a crime committed, and if so, did a specific person commit the crime?" Essentially, this means that the cop only has to have a 51% belief that a crime was committed and a 51% belief that you committed it, again a very easy standard, but harder than "Reasonable Suspicion."

SO NOW WHAT?

Now, the cop does one of two things, issues you a citation, or places you under arrest. Now you might think, 'Oops, now I am screwed.' Not necessarily. If your arrest is legitimate, and not contrived, which we will cover a little later, now the technicalities that lawyers are infamous for come into play. The first is "Chain of Custody", which means that the cop has to bag and tag your pot into evidence and be able to prove in court, that the bag was not tampered with, and that the contents thereof have not been altered in any way. Before trial, when your lawyer receives Discovery, which is a fancy way of saying that your lawyer is entitled to all of the evidence that will be used against you, your lawyer will review the Chain of Custody. If there are any errors, then your lawyer will move to suppress the evidence at trial. While it might seem straightforward, most police forces are overwhelmed with criminal cases, and much of the time they do not bother to follow proper procedure for minor crimes like pot possession.

Let's say, that the signatures on the evidence bag, match the ones on the intake property sheet for the evidence locker, and except for the cop and the property custodian no one else was involved in handling the evidence.

GUESS WHAT?

It will be admitted into evidence. So the first technical hurdle is over, but the next one is actually pretty useful. The cop has to prove that the "Green Leafy Substance" is actually marijuana and not something that is not illegal. Sadly, many judges let the cops substantiate their statement that the pot is actually pot based upon their "Training and Experience", so if it walks, talks and looks like a proverbial duck, it probably is one. However, there are some judges that still stick to the rules of evidence, and will not allow the cop to testify that what you were arrested with is actually marijuana.

This is when your lawyer starts to really earn their money, demanding to see the lab report showing that the evidence was tested and came back as pot. No lab reports, game over, you go home. If there is a lab report, then your lawyer will insist that the laboratory technician who did the tests which determined that you had marijuana on you, appear in court, where your lawyer will cross-examine the technician on lots of technical procedures. By the way, the Chain of Custody issue will come back again, as now the pot has left the police evidence locker, gone to the state lab, and come back again. So your lawyer will get another bite at this apple.

What this does is increase the chance that your pot can be "Suppressed" or not admitted into evidence. If there is no evidence of an actual crime, again, you get to go home. If the evidence is admitted into court, then your last hope, and it's a slim one, is to argue that it was not your pot. Now everyone will say that it is not their pot, and the judge or jury rarely believe you, especially if it is found in your purse, or in your pocket. The argument that you were "holding it" for someone else will not work, as possession, literally means that an object was in your actual control.

However, if you get stopped for speeding because you have been doing bong hits all day, and the cop smells the odor of marijuana on you, he can ask you to exit the vehicle and submit to roadside sobriety tests to see if you are Driving While Intoxicated (DWI). Most people think that DWI, or its identical cousin Driving Under the Influence of an Intoxicating Substance, only concerns alcohol. Nothing could be farther from the truth. The actual crime is whether or not your driving was impaired to the slightest degree by anything. By anything, I mean that literally, examples are booze, street drugs, prescription painkillers, antihistamines, cough syrup, and probably coffee if they really wanted to bother. So, if he smells weed on you, he can ask you to do the roadside tests, which are incredibly difficult to get right as they are all balance and coordination tests. Thankfully, weed makes most people sluggish rather than stumble, so most of the time; you don't get arrested for DWI. No arrest, you get back in your car, insist that your speeding ticket goes to court, and off you go.

However, if you get arrested, then the cop is allowed to search your car and find your stash, during his inventory of your vehicle. Without an arrest, he can only search your car if he sees any evidence of pot, such as a joint burning in the ashtray, or that the weed is in plain sight. Plain sight means, literally that, the cop looks through the windows of your car and sees a "Green Leafy Substance" on the seat next to you; you get your pot possession ticket/arrest.

If there is nothing in plain sight, then the Cop may ask you for permission to search your vehicle. **DO NOT ALLOW THE COP A VOLUNTARY SEARCH!!** If it's under your seat, in your trunk, in a backpack, or anywhere else where it's not in plain sight, you are good to go. If you give the cop permission to search your vehicle, you abandon all of your Constitutional Rights against Unreasonable Search and Seizure. So, to reiterate one of the earliest things I said in this book, be honest with the cop about speeding, weaving, or other minor moving violations so that you might get out of the ticket in the first place, but if have drugs, open containers of alcohol, weapons, or a 15-year-old hot teen runaway in your car, you do not let them search it. If they take you out of the vehicle without arresting you, and you don't give them permission to search your vehicle, whatever they find is inadmissible. As I said above, if there is no evidence of a crime, there will not be a conviction.

WHAT ABOUT PLANTING EVIDENCE?

This does not happen in pot possession cases, it really does not, unless you have got a cop that is just plain dirty, and has weed in his vehicle. Why doesn't it happen? Because small amounts of weed and possession tickets have few serious consequences, and they do not do much to pad the cops arrest statistics.

What does happen, however, is the fact that cops do make "Pretextual Stops" of people that they think are up to no good.

WHAT IS PRETEXTUAL STOP?

A stop where there is no evidence that there is anything wrong with your vehicle, with you're driving, or if you are walking, that you are walking like a normal person. The easiest way for the cops to do this is to run your vehicle's license plate through the cop's computer system to check if there are any warrants out for you. If so, you are going to get stopped. Most jurisdictions will not allow the cops to randomly run someone's license plate, "fishing" for warrants. There needs to be another reason, so this is when the pretext happens, and here are a few examples:

a.Broken Tail Light, or broken License Plate Light when they are both working.

b.Current Registration sticker on your license plate, which they allegedly can't see.

c.Excessive noise or smoke coming from your vehicle, both completely subjective.

d.Window tint that they say is legally too dark when it actually isn't.

e.That they thought that they saw you on your cell phone.

f.Because you were a minority in a white neighborhood or driving a beater that the cops didn't think belonged wherever you were.

So, if there was no objective evidence that you were speeding, weaving, etc., then your lawyer will do their best to show that the cop should not have stopped you in the first place. If your lawyer wins this argument, then you go home, if not, then everything that I have talked about in this chapter starts to happen to you.

HOW DO YOU AVOID BEING ARRESTED FOR POT POSSESSION?

Easy, don't smoke it if it's illegal in your state. But, if you do smoke your pot, smoke it inside the house, in the bathroom under the exhaust fan, that way, if the cops come to your house with a noise complaint from your stereo where you are blasting "Dark Side of the Moon" at deafening volume, they will not smell any pot. Pink Floyd, the Grateful Dead, any Reggae artist particularly Bob Marley, are some of the artists most listened to when pulling bong hits by the way.

Next, if you are transporting your weed, keep it in your trunk inside of a closed container, so that is not in plain sight if you get stopped. Try and avoid driving while stoned, because while you will see in the next book in this series, which is all about DWI, getting convicted of being high on weed is really difficult to prove, it gives the cops reasonable suspicion to pat you down if you get stopped. Finally, keep all of your pot in one plastic bag, do not have it divided up into smaller quantities so that it looks like you are not just in possession of the weed, but you are going to sell it.

Now, if you have it divided up for sale, please for the love of God do not have it sitting next to a digital jewelry scale, and small bills to make change, otherwise, you will be paying your lawyer a lot more money to get you out of "Trafficking a Controlled Substance", or in layman's terms, "Dealing". Dealing, which is covered in another book, is almost always a Felony, which means serious consequences for you.

In conclusion, try and be sensible about your habits and your addictions, while I know that for most of you this is probably an oxymoron (aka contradiction in terms). But seriously, you have a few more rights to do something stupid in your car than you do walking around in public, as most jurisdictions have ruled that your car is an extension of your home. As I have said above, however, the cops can get around these restrictions if you are driving around much of the time.

Your home, to use the well-worn phrase, is your castle, and unless the cops can see, hear or smell an obvious crime occurring, they need a search warrant to enter and search your home.

IF THEY KNOCK ON YOUR DOOR WITHOUT A WARRANT AND ASK IF THEY CAN COME IN, WHAT IS YOUR ANSWER?

No, I am sorry, but no. You don't need to be rude about it, but again, once you let them into your house/apartment, even a room rented out in someone else's house, anything that they can see in plain sight can and will be used against you in a court of law. So again, don't let the cops into your house, and do not under any circumstances allow them to search your place without a warrant.

Finally, I have an excellent example of how and why the location of abusing your favorite substance makes all the difference in the world. You can read about the following encounter in its full ridiculous detail, in my first memoir, "Expensive Janitor", but here is the abridged version.

Trixie, my client, was a stripper who liked to go to her neighborhood park, after it was closed, sit on a bench and smoke her pot. She did this three Monday nights in a row and got 3 pot possession citations in a row. When I had worked out a miracle of a deal, Trixie was foolish enough to ask the judge, "When can I go to the park and smoke my pot and not get arrested?" The Judge had a great sense of humor and responded, "While it's still illegal, you might try smoking your pot at home and then go to the park." Sadly, that made Trixie very happy and also illustrates my point. Keep your bad habits at home and you will probably not darken my doorstep in need of my help.

CHAPTER 8

TRAFFIC TICKETS WHERE YOU DON'T NEED A LAWYER

REMARKABLY, there are some traffic tickets that you can resolve yourself, and these are simple and straightforward, the first of which is Defective Equipment. Defective equipment reads just like it sounds:

a. You have something wrong with your vehicle, such as a headlight, tail light, or license plate light that has gone out.

b. Your car is billowing huge clouds of smoke.

c. Your windows were tinted darker than they are allowed to be.

The solution for this is easy; fix your beater so that you do not get stopped again! Then, when it's time for your court date, you simply present proof to the cop and the judge that you got your car fixed, and that there is no longer a problem. Unless these tickets were added to something actually involving your driving, you are home and dry as the Brits like to say, with no court costs, fines, or points.

The next tickets are no registration and no insurance. No registration is easy to fix, just get your car registered, and take proof of it to court, simply say that you forgot to renew it, and even if your registration has been expired for months, you will probably walk away. At worst, you will get a small fine, no points, and no jail. It is cheaper to just fix this without one of us holding your hand.

No Insurance can be easy to fix, depending on the State that you are in. New Mexico is one of the few states that does not give someone jail time, or impound their car just because they did not have insurance. Economically, New Mexico is an incredibly impoverished state, the poorest in the country. Worse, it is geographically a huge state, meaning that lots of people have to drive a vehicle to get anywhere, public transportation is horrible in Albuquerque, and virtually non-existent anywhere else. So, politically, the State Legislators, do not want to be seen as "Criminalizing the Poor", or in other words, jailing one of their broke ass constituents for being too poor to have the mandatory minimum liability insurance on their car. If the person is too poor to insure their vehicle, or they have too many points, they are probably well behind on their child support payments, don't have a job, moved back in with their mom, or some other poverty-related situation.

If you are in New Mexico, and your insurance lapses, you need to get insurance and take the insurance card to court with you and hope that the cop or the judge will let you off. They usually will, as the goal is to have every driver insured, and with New Mexico being the least insured state in the United States, every person that can be seen to have valid insurance, even if it's only one month, gets off pretty easily. Even if you get convicted of no insurance, the worst that is going to happen to you the first time is a $100.00 fine, and a lecture from the judge. I have never seen a judge in over two decades of practice put someone in jail for no insurance, or even impose community service. No Insurance does not involve an offense related to your driving, it carries no points.

There are severe penalties for not having insurance if you cause an accident. You will be stuck paying for the damage to the other person's car, and their injuries if any. Worse, if the person that you hit has comprehensive Insurance on their car, their insurer will chase you for the money that you owe them. If you do not pay, then they are allowed to file a lawsuit demanding their money. Presuming you are too poor to pay it, then they will get a judgment against you, and have the Motor Vehicle Division suspend your license until you pay them off.

Other jurisdictions may be stricter, and you may face points or jail time, so call a traffic attorney first to see what the penalties are for not having insurance. If they tell you that you can take care of it on your own, then follow their advice and save yourself some money. If they tell you that you are facing jail or points on your license, go get yourself a lawyer.

CHAPTER 9
CONCLUSION

First, I want to thank you for buying and reading this book, I hope that it has been interesting and helpful regarding whatever situation you have found yourself in. If you didn't need this book but you bought it out of curiosity, chances are you will need this information some day and my book will come in handy.

Let's go over a few of the points that I have made repetitively in this book so that you do not forget.

First, the cop has a ton of discretion about what tickets they give you and how bad they might be. Be polite and apologetic, and if it's something minor like speeding, admit that you were wrong, and you might just not need me. If it's a more serious offense, be polite and apologetic, but do not admit to the charge, just say that you were not paying attention. While Driver Inattention carries 2 points in New Mexico, it's a lot better to get this on your record rather than a Careless or Reckless Driving citation.

Second, Get a Lawyer! Unless it's no registration or broken tail light, you should have realized by now that the money you pay us is well spent, and at the end of the process, hiring one of us is probably the best thing that you can do. This is particularly important if you commit an offense that will lead to automatic jail time (Evading or Eluding), automatic loss of your license (Reckless Driving), prohibition of getting a loan for college (Pot Possession), or worst of all, Divorce (Solicitation of a Prostitute). Trust me, on this, except for the tickets that I mentioned in the previous chapter, if you get stopped and get a ticket, you will need one of us to clean up your mess. This last sentence is the reason that my memoir is entitled "Expensive Janitor", as sadly this is what most lawyers are.

If you have enjoyed this book look for forthcoming books in this series, look for more of my books that delve into more serious criminal offenses, personal injury cases, contracts and leases, and wills and estates.

Finally, if it's not too much trouble, please post a short review on Amazon, Goodreads, or any other place that you might have bought this book. Reviews are critically important, good or bad, for authors and help us market our books more effectively than any advertising campaign. Thanks again for reading, and I will see you in the next book!

Lightning Source UK Ltd.
Milton Keynes UK
UKHW010953280820
368951UK00004B/157